Dirty Verse

Dirty Verse Publishing LLC
Lewisville, Pennsylvania
www.dirtyverse.xyz
@dirtyversexyz

Printed in the United States of America

Library of Congress Control Number: 2025920224

ISBN: 979-8-9998361-0-6

Sordid. Raw. Unabashed. Relentless.

Content Warning:

This book contains material that may trigger any and every possible sensitivity that exists and may ever exist.

You have been forewarned.

Warning: You *__will__* be offended by the contents of this book.

This is a collection of rhyming poetry that crosses all lines of decorum. Some poems in this book will not offend everyone, but . . . ***Every*** poem in this book will offend someone.

The list of likely offendees (not exhaustive): *Women, Men, Blacks, Whites, Hispanics, Asians, Aliens, Democrats, Republicans, woke-ists, MAGA-ists, cisgender, binary, transsexuals, homosexuals, homophobes, dead people, cannibals, animal lovers, damsels in distress, heroes seeking to save damsels in distress, mothers, fathers, grandparents, elderly people, youthful people, war veterans, the clergy, anyone with any medical condition ever discovered, ugly people, pretty people, fairy godmothers, little people/midgets/dwarfs, world leaders, alcoholics, astronomers, deaf people, blind people, celebrities, pornstars, writers who have actual talent, teachers, Americans, un-Americans, non-Americans, neanderthals, geniuses, idiots, royalty, Santa Claus, bald people, barbers, circus freaks, cloned people, gravediggers, necrophiliacs, mourners, dentists, Taylor Swift, degenerate gamblers, drug addicts, law enforcement officials, circus performers, alien abductees, artists and illustrators.*

The List of Infractions

Part 1
Brilliant Social Statements

Sans Redeeming Qualities

Morality Check

There once was a young giraffe
Who felt that he didn't belong
Because the animals liked to laugh
At his neck, which was quite long.

He was left all alone;
No one would be his friend,
Because his neck had grown
And now would not descend.

As they played, he would imagine
Frolicking in the sunshine.
He'd ask them if he could join in,
But they always declined.

Then one day the ground froze
And the animals' food did freeze,
But the giraffe's neck just rose
To the leaves up in the trees.

All of the animals pleaded
For the giraffe to keep them alive
By giving the food they needed
So that they could survive.

He saw their consternation
And the tears that were in each eye.
And he felt their desperation,
As he watched them starve and die.

Dead Frogs Don't Ribbit

Few things in life are certain,
But one thing that I do know
Is that dead frogs don't ribbit
And dead flowers never grow.

When an apple falls from its tree
It soon is rotten to the core,
And when Bozo came to his end
He became a dreadful bore.

And since my nuisance neighbor
Got run over by my car,
During that parking incident,
He's been less annoying by far.

Once a thing's no longer living
I've found it rarely acts the same,
So ever since my grandpa bit it
My birthday gifts aren't quite so lame.

But I'll buck that trend when I go
And my epitaph's arranged,
Whence it reads, "He did nothing in life,
So, in death, he will be unchanged."

Trouble in the Kitchen

The pot called the kettle black
And the kettle was offended.
He thought it was a racial attack,
Causing a rift that went unmended.

The kettle had the pot arrested
For his slanderous remark.
And the pot angrily protested,
Saying, "That kettle *is* quite dark!"

Because the kettle was boiling mad
The pot spent the night in prison,
For the kettle had just been darkly clad,
Which was seen once the sun had risen.

“A color is color and nothing more,"
Is the moral this story detailed.
So let us succeed ever more
Where the pot and the kettle have failed.

Legendary War Heroes?

Once upon a time,
So the legend goes,
Some men did some fighting.
Over what? No one knows.

Their battle was epic,
Though the details are blurred,
So, we don't know its length
Or when it occurred.

Nor does anyone know
The name of this war
Or where it took place,
Whether land, sea, or shore.

All the soldiers were brave
And earned their great fame.
At least we guess they did,
Since we don't know their names.

All that we can say
Is that their war's done
And that they're now dead,
Though we don't know who won.

Non-Prophet

Just like the Greek, Cassandra,
Who knew, but wasn't believed,
When I tell people their future,
Their responses are preconceived.

The fundamental difference
Is they *believe* each word I say
And adjust their lives according to
The foolish thoughts that I convey.

If I said the world exploded
While we were all standing there
They'd say something like "*What a shame!*
But how nice of you to care."

That would be all well and good
If clairvoyance was my trade.
But since I'm just making stuff up
Nothing I say should be obeyed.

My hope is that the day will come
When no "truth" comes from my mind,
And I can be a fool again
With no impact on mankind.

Reading Material

The walls of public bathrooms
Hold stalls of communication
Where brilliant minds disseminate
Their genius for generations.

They will glimpse immortality
As their art stands time's test
To compare to the greatest thinkers
The world has seen from east to west.

And so it begins:

Bathroom stall Shakespeare
Expresses via sonnet
The desire for his manhood
To have someone's mouth upon it.

Bathroom stall Picasso,
With the flair of his brush,
Illustrates with great detail
What is done, but not flushed.

Bathroom stall Freud,
Writes with both ego and id,
About his raging libido
And sordid things my mom did.

Bathroom stall Einstein,
With his relative theory,
Writes about his half-sister
With a closeness that's eerie.

Bathroom stall MLK
Did indeed have a dream
Involving black and white people,
And, it seems, flavored whipped cream.

By pen, spray can, or carving knife
And all other tools of their trade
These clandestine prodigies
Carry out their useless crusade.

Incognito in the Name of Beauty

A nip here, a tuck there
And dermal filling space;
Soon not even your mom
Would recognize your face.

Suctions, Botox, implants
Were your pathway to success.
Just a couple more "-plasty's"
And you're certain to impress.

You lived life for this moment,
To at last become a star.
The only problem being
That no one knows who you are.

Anyone can get a job,
The trick's living without one.
And anyone can exercise,
But those people are no fun.

It's much harder to sleep all day
Than it is to be productive.
I'd actually say that doing things
Can sometimes be quite destructive.

Some people choose to take head-on
The challenges life may bring.
My approach is somewhat different,
As I choose not to do a thing.

I consider it "zagging"
When everyone chooses to zig.
Someday the world will come around
And I will make it very big.

But before that day, I'll rest up,
Not wanting to overextend.
Oh, by the way, I meant to ask
If you have a few bucks to lend?

Part 2
Let's grab your attention

with a bit of Sex & Violence

Dream Girl

I found the girl of my dreams
While I was asleep,
But sadly, this girl, it seems,
Was one I could not keep.

For she lived beneath my eyelids,
And outside she wasn't real.
Once I found this out I did
Try to cop a feel.

I figured, "What could she do?
She is just in my mind."
And with this thought that I knew
I reached for her behind.

I was stopped before I got there
By my dream girl's eyes.
She gave me the coldest stare
Then kicked between my thighs.

I then imagined great pain
And awakened with a wince.
I had just a minor sprain,
But I've not slept well since.

Undying Love

My girl and I, beneath our star,
Set up our picnic basket.
I had arrived in my car
And she came in her casket.

It seems she'd died some time ago,
Though after we'd made our date,
But I exhumed her body so
That she would not be late.

I spread the blanket on the ground
And propped her against a tree,
And though her face only frowned
It was a smile to me.

We ate a lot — at least *I* did —
And drank cheap wine from France.
She winked her decomposed eyelid,
Prompting intimate romance.

But throughout these moments of bliss
I realized that I couldn't keep
This girlfriend corpse, so after a kiss
I put her back six feet deep.

That Bell Don't Unring

A man chose to change his gender,
Which is perfectly fine to do,
But is something to be sure of
Before making the switcheroo.

This man in particular
Had never sought women to date,
So, he thought a change of sides
Would make everything great.

But post-surgery, she wondered,
With her newfound intuition,
If perhaps a love for women
Might be her new condition.

Since she'd had this change of heart,
But couldn't again change her sex,
She figured her best alternative
Was a love that's a bit more complex.

It was hard enough telling his friends
He was a man attracted to men,
But then she became a woman
To come out of the closet again.

The Biggest Lie of All

Much like that doll, Pinocchio,
I cannot tell any lies,
Or my nose will start to grow
Beyond its normal size.

My nose expands when I say
Anything that might deceive,
Which is a fact I learned the hard way
Sometime late last Christmas Eve.

It seems that I had forgotten
To get a gift for my girl.
So, I gave her a box of cotton
Then was "shocked" by the missing pearl.

I insisted that it had been there
And that there was no explanation,
At least not one that I could share
While maintaining our relations.

Then I knew I'd been found out
By my girlfriend super sleuth.
She cried and began to shout
And begged me to tell the truth.

But I just continued lying,
Until my nose could grow no more.
Despite my constant denying
My nose was too big to ignore.

She left me later that day,
Until I brought her some roses
And asked, "Don't you know what they say
About guys who have big noses?"

Then her return was no surprise,
Nor was her requesting of
My telling her twenty-five lies
Prior to our making love.

Binge Size Matters

After a late-night drinking
I put my beer goggles on,
Then saw a girl and started thinking,
"I'd bet she'll look good come dawn."

So, I made my approach
And trotted out my best line,
"Would you like your breakfast eggs poached
Or will you just have some of mine?"

It nearly shocked me sober
When she didn't smack my face,
So I started to disrobe her
And headed for second base.

She seemed quite eager to go
So we hopped into a cab.
I felt something starting to grow
About when she started to grab.

The back seat was getting so hot
The cabbie nearly wrecked the car,
But I still tipped him a lot
Because I was getting so far.

Now, generally I don't boast,
But I had this girl so in heat
That I quick notched my bed post
Before we were under the sheet.

But once we finally were
I was quite surprised to find
That the penis she had on her
Was at least twice the size of mine.

Men With Dragon-Slaying Prowess Get All the Chicks

The monster's nostrils flared
And the flames shot toward me.
I turned to the large beast and stared,
In hopes that he would flee.

I pulled my sword from its sheath
Then called him to come near.
That's when I saw his sharp teeth,
Which produced a lot of fear.

My body started quaking,
So I thought I'd give a warning.
"It may look like I'm shaking,
But you'd best be gone by morning."

But the dragon marched ahead,
Toward *me*, the dragon slayer.
Perhaps I could have stabbed him dead,
But instead, I said a prayer.

I then let out a loud shrill.
I shuddered and shied away.
That's when I heroically killed –
Or at least that's what they say.

For as he made his advance
He slipped on the tears I'd cried
And was impaled, quite by chance,
On the sword lying by my side.

The Perils of a Sideshow Freak Avocation

The sword swallower swallowed the sword,
Which was wonderful, his partner assured,

Except for the problem that could not be ignored,
Which was the wound from where the blood poured,

The details of which a doctor explored
And asked, "He *meant* to swallow the sword?"

He then sent him to a mental ward
And wrote on his chart, which hung on a board,

"Gored by a sword and out of his gourd."

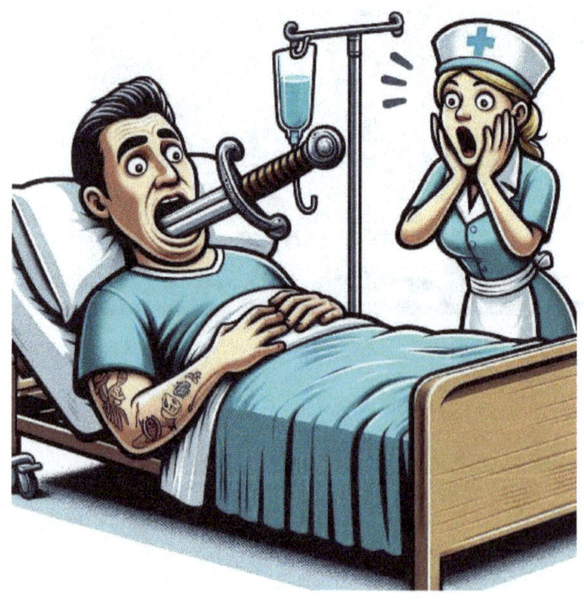

Pyromania Has Its Place in Society

Mommy came home loaded,
So I turned the gas on,
Lit the match, she exploded.
And then mommy was gone.

The funeral was sad.
Then they buried charred mom,
While I wondered if Dad
Could diffuse a time bomb.

Well, needless to say
He quite clearly could not,
And so, the next day,
He took the adjacent plot.

A foster home took me
But I was gone in two days,
Shrouded in the mystery
Of that four-alarm blaze.

So, tomorrow in court
It's me versus the State,
And since my fuse is short
It will be a *hot* date.

Casualty of Love

Last night, beneath your balcony,
I stood before you on one knee

And sang to you your favorite song
To let you know that I was wrong

And wanted to apologize
For telling you all of those lies,

When someone tossed a live grenade,
Interrupting my serenade.

When I heard machine gun fire,
It somewhat quelled my desire.

But as all of the bullets flew
I still could only think of you,

Until I saw that it was thee
That was waging war against me.

I must admit it made me sad
To know you want me dead that bad.

I hope this won't become a trend
That my love for you, you want to end.

If You Give a Pornstar Pudding

If you give a pornstar pudding
She'll likely think it's something else,
And then she'll ask to be paid
To use lubricants and gels.

If you pay a pornstar
She'll probably come back for more,
Glad to provide her services
In the bedroom or on the floor.

If a pornstar provides service
There's a good chance she'll rock your world,
Putting a big smile on your face
That won't be easily unfurled.

If a pornstar rocks your world
You'll both work up quite a thirst,
Which will lead her to raid your fridge,
Since you're asleep and finished first.

If a pornstar raids your fridge
I'd bet she'll want something to eat.
And after a quick round two
She'll get herself a pudding treat.

Bad Boyfriend (Gets What He Deserves)

Her boyfriend cheats at checkers
While she astounds in chess.
He pisses on the toilet seat
But never will confess.

He drinks her paycheck weekly
With friends at the local bar.
He says that he'd invite her,
But they only have one car.

He doesn't really have a job –
That work thing can be quite hard.
Besides, she has a nice house
With a pool and ample yard.

She was a top graduate
While he was the class clown.
She's always there to lift him up
But he only puts her down.

He's useless in every way.
He doesn't have any skill.
Though he'd never come to her aid
When he needs her, she surely will.

But there's something he doesn't know,
Which explains why she doesn't mind,
And tolerates his nonsense –
He's the fifth boyfriend of his kind.

She certainly has a type –
Someone of whom no one will care
When she buries him in the backyard
With the other deadbeats to spare.

The Untimely Demise of Chivalry

Your violent muscle spasm,
Which I couldn't help mistaking
For just another orgasm
That you were skillfully faking,

Had left you there immobile,
With a back that wouldn't bend,
And though I should have been noble
I instead made that our end.

I had been seeking the chance
To break up for a year.
But made it so after a glance
At your nurse's ample rear.

Besides, your tears and sobbing voice
Was somewhat unappealing,
Which left me with little choice
But to give in to the feeling.

Perhaps I shouldn't have asked her out
Before I had left your space,
But did you really have to shout
And throw your pee bag in my face?

It seems you'll be laid up a while,
So, I'll be on my way.
Next time, I hope you're less hostile
And we'll call it light foreplay.

Part 3
Tales from a Properly

Dysfunctional Family *(Pets Included)*

Dinner is Serviced

Mommy once said it's lunchtime
And laid me across her lap.
I suckled from her nipple
And afterwards took a nap.

She said, "You're getting older.
Time may come to stop feeding."
But when I whined and cried
She gave in to my pleading.

She now protests daily,
But my cries force a trickle.
Perhaps I'll shave my beard,
To free her from the tickle.

Flush Attack

A lukewarm morning shower
Helps me to start the day,
As the water's soothing rhythm
Take my aches and pains away.

But when left all alone
With a vindictive spouse
There is no place to hide
In what is just one house.

So, what were peaceful moments
Quickly take an awful turn
When the lever is depressed
And I feel the scalding burn.

You learn a lesson each day.
Just a fool must learn it twice.
So now, before I shower
I'm the epitome of nice.

Insanity is Relative

Uncle Lou and Aunt Jane,
Because they're insane,
Become werewolves each Halloween.
They shave their dog's hair
And glue it where they're bare
And make gestures that I find obscene.

My strange Cousin Betty
Proudly eats spaghetti
Without using a fork or spoon.
Ever since she was young
She's just scooped with her tongue,
While humming her favorite tune.

My nephew with no name,
Whom my brother won't claim
To have ever seen before,
Has seventeen toes
And a three-holed nose,
Which the doctors can't seem to cure.

Dad's fighting a war,
That was done long before,
Because he was hurt during his.
So, 1995
Will always be alive –
At least for as long as he is.

Granny's the queen nut
Because she sticks her butt
On what she thinks is a flying broom.
A witch she is not,
But it explains a lot
About descendants from her womb.

Man Cave Makeover

I used to watch football
Relaxed with some beers.
Then I got married
And things changed through the years.

From dart board and posters
And superhero capes
To flowers, scented oils
And candles and drapes.

When our daughter was born
She cried during the games
And my wife screamed at *me*
When I yelled out bad names.

Then a second child came
And, though I sure pleaded,
"Some play space for the kids,"
Is what the room needed.

With child number three
The pool table vanished,
Which made me wonder
If *I'd* soon be banished.

With the birth of a fourth
My Sunday space became
A sticky, soaked couch
With a juice box to blame.

So now I watch football
In a quite crowded place,
But I still find I do so
With a smile on my face.

Parents Just Don't Understand

I was born last month
To a mom and a dad
Who seem to be nice,
But they're hearing's gone bad.

I tell them what I need –
And I'm perfectly clear.
But mom and dad act
Like they can't even hear.

When I point and I talk
They seem to understand,
But then bring the wrong thing
Or just wipe off my hand.

When they ask a question
I respond right away,
But if I ask one of them
They seem confused all day.

The one thing I've noticed
Is they seem to be new.
So perhaps they're still learning
What to say and to do.

But if they don't get it.
And I'm left at a loss.
Perhaps relaxed bowels
Will get my point across.

Squatting Toddlers

Several destitute beggars
Have overrun my home –
They ransacked all the rooms.
And smashed a garden gnome.

They go weeks without bathing,
And often don't comb their hair.
If I suggest that they should
They make it clear they don't care.

They can't read or write.
They act like unlearned fools.
They're unhelpful most times
And defiant of rules.

These filthy, short people
With poor bathroom demeanor,
Nearly staged a full coup
When asked to be cleaner.

They have been here for years,
Freeloading food and drink.
And with nowhere to go
I teeter on the brink.

Though I guess you could say
That I, in part, bear the blame,
Since they were born into this
And each have my last name.

The Elephant in the Room

No matter your issue –
How troubling it seems –
And how it may crush
All your hopes and dreams.

And though no one helps
Or speaks of your pain
And prance around it,
ignoring the strain,

It doesn't compare
To the troubling dread
Of a pachyderm daily
Sleeping next to my bed.

And when I awake?
Well, he's no nomad,
So, he's here all the time
And it smells pretty bad.

He's blocking the door
So, I can't ever depart.
So, imagine my fear
That he may someday fart.

This is My Cat (Beside the Moose's Head)

My cross-eyed cat
Never caught a rat
Because she always seemed to forget
That when the dogs howl
It meant they're on the prowl,
So she was the pussy they'd get.

And her meow was so meek
She would not eat for a week
Because I would forget she was there.
Thanks to her feeble purr
I even once vacuumed her
Thinking she was a big clump of hair.

And though she was pretty
I punished my kitty
For that last litter catastrophe.
If she'd gone in the box
Instead of on my socks
I wouldn't now have a cat ass trophy.

Rabbitation

I left my two pet rabbits
Alone for a little while
And I returned, curious to find
That each was sporting a smile.

I left my ten pet rabbits
Alone for a little while
And I returned, curious to find
That each was sporting a smile.

I left my fifty pet rabbits
Alone for a little while
And I returned, curious to find
That each was sporting a smile.

I left my three hundred rabbits
Alone for a little while
And I returned, *less* curious to find
Each one placed in caged exile.

Retirement Village Mysteries: The Case of the Missing Purse Dog

Elsie took her dog everywhere
Until she woke up this morning
And found her friend nowhere around –
She was gone without a warning.

"Cuddles!" she screamed throughout the hall,
Awakening every resident.
"Please, someone call the police,
"Or the mayor or the President."

There was a dog napper among them
Was the breakfast room scuttlebutt.
And what might happen to Cuddles?
Would she be treated as if a mutt?

I thought there was more to the story.
Everything else was still in its place.
How could a dog have vanished
Without leaving the slightest trace?

Then I heard a neighbor chatting
And eavesdropped just to probe.
She had just come from her spa day
And swore Cuddles was wearing a robe.

I glanced around the room again
To prove that it was no rumor,
And found a note fallen to the ground
Which read, "*Took Cuddles to the groomer.*"

Horrors from the Closet

The closet couldn't hold
Them back anymore.
The pressure just mounted,
Till they broke down the door.

Now they're under the bed
Or at the foot of the stairs,
And at night can be found
Nearly everywhere.

Some are thin, some are thick
And some reach to my thighs,
Though overall most
Are about the same size.

If not for my fear
I would stand to oppose
This population
As it tragically grows,

But the repercussions
Far exceed my just cause,
So instead of action,
I can only pause.

So, you ask if it's
Monsters on the loose?
Oh no, just my wife's
Collection of shoes.

They've consumed my life
From sandal to suede boot.
I can only hope my
Daughters don't follow suit.

The Underappreciated Companionship of Zombie Rats

I asked my superintendent
To consider a lower rent
Because of the small issue that
I live with undead rodents.

He called it a "special feature."
One no other unit could boast,
Suggesting *I* was the problem,
And could be a more gracious host.

So, I took his feedback to heart,
Ignoring their dropped fecal matter,
With a gesture and peace offering
Of a fresh kill pig brain platter.

Now we all get along quite well
And I have no reason to worry,
Since whenever they give chase
They invariably need to scurry.

Junk Male

She sought out a decent guy,
But got a string of creeps.
No one worthy of her time
Let alone to have for keeps.

What about a mail-order man?
She thought about in her mind.
One she could order as desired:
Good looking, smart, and kind.

She placed an order quickly
And he showed up in two weeks,
But she noted a drooling tick
And body odor that reeked.

She went back onto the website
And read "*No Returns*" in fine print,
While her new man slept in snoring,
His bad breath in need of mint.

She then placed an ad of her own,
Describing a life of leisure,
And sold this newfound bachelor,
Turning a profit for good measure.

Part 4
The Quick & The Dirty

The Tragic Consequence of Poor Urinal Etiquette

There once was a guy
With a roving left eye,
Which caused his untimely demise,
For he looked down below
Where a brawny hick stood to go
And then commented on his size.

And the Rose-Colored Glass is Half-Full

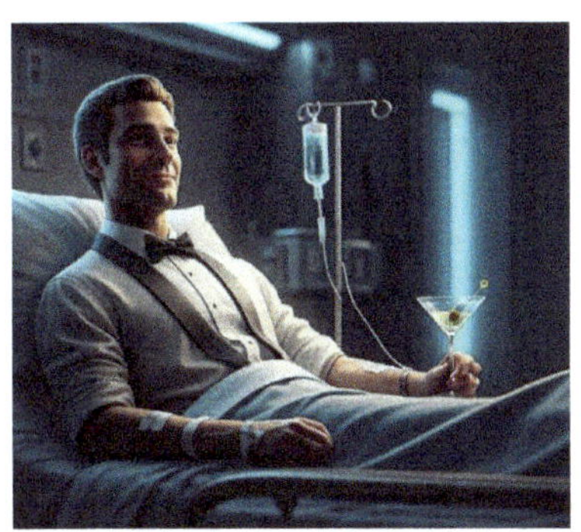

The hospital trip
Caused by a heartbeat's skip
Could, with ease, ruin one's day,
But another sip
From the morphine drip
Makes for a quite pleasant stay.

Condom Supernova

Tequila impaired judgment
And a phallic giraffe balloon
Inevitably conclude with
Parenthood far too soon.

Picked Clean

A nose-picker knows
That a picked nose blows
With tremendous freedom and ease.
But an *over-picked* nose,
Where membranes decompose,
May be a bloody mess when you sneeze.

Erectile Dissed Function

Given my fetish for heavy-set women
And that I heard someone shout, "Meaty Whore!"
You can imagine my disappointment
To look up at that streaking meteor.

Fool in a Crowd

I began the flash mob sing-song,
But I knew that something was wrong.
Since I didn't know the words
I sang something absurd
And no one could sing along.

The Cannibal Diner

Nothing could be finer
Than the Cannibal Diner
If you have a taste for flesh.
You can eat if you choose,
Or for cocktails transfuse,
And the menu is always fresh.

"It's Curtains for You"

An old-time gangster meets a seamstress
In a window treatment facility.
When she's done and hands him the package
She states this obvious fait accompli.

Body Shop

His muscles are flexed and oiled.
His Speedo is tight and small,
Which looks great for a contest,
But not at the shopping mall.

Piss and Venom

A jumping spider army
I hope to never see.
But if I do, I'll warn you
My pants, I'll surely pee.

Testing Gravity

In retrospect, perhaps,
A cinder block as a tool
Was not the best solution
For testing Sir Isaac's rule,

But four broken toes
That, in hindsight, I'd expect,
I think prove his theory
Was exactly correct.

The Importance of Proper Enunciation

My bombastic flatulent emission,
Which disrupted Geology class,
Was not the answer the teacher sought
When he asked about volcanic *ash*.

Whole-ly Cow

It used to be an expression
That I used to convey surprise,
But the script was flipped on that
When I saw one with my own eyes.

The Great Guzzler

As superhero traits go
Mine is least impressive of all,
But if you need a keg drained
I'm the crusader to call.

Part 5
The Effects of Drinking

& Drug Use

The Aftermath of Attempted Suicide by Hallucinogen

I lay down on my deathbed,
So I could finally get some sleep,
But I got no rest, no peace, instead
I lay there counting those damn sheep.

There was no white light beckoning.
I could not find Heaven's Gate.
It seemed no day of reckoning
Was meant for my eternal fate.

Those sheep kept jumping the fence –
A tireless, continuous fleet –
Disrupting my humble reverence
With their "baas" and shuffling feet.

Their ubiquitous presence
Has kept me living many more years
Than was my intended existence,
And there's no end in sight, it appears.

A Man's True Love

The joy of your smile is delighting
As is your head in my lap,
But it can't surpass how exciting
It is to find out what's on tap.

So tonight, I must depart thee,
Against my pained heart's will,
Because, though I know you love me,
There's much beer for me to swill.

For the only way to replace
The tender warmth of your hug
Is with the heartfelt embrace
Of another frosty mug.

So, while sucking from the bottle's top
Down at the local beer hall
I'll think of you while my tears drop
At the shouting of "Last call!"

So "cheers" to you, my darling dear,
And "cheers" to the guy over there,
Who bought several pints of beer
For everyone to share.

Super High Fly Demigod

Last night's nuclear assault
On the western hemisphere
Was not a foreign power's fault,
But that of a case of beer.

For as my buzz was kicking in
And "beer guts" were in excess
I did the thing called heroin,
That has called this awful mess.

I pumped that junk into my vein
Then convulsed till almost dawn,
Then launched missiles and drank champagne,
And "Bombs away!" our country's gone.

I was my own superpower,
Smiling through each detonation.
As I got higher by the hour,
So did the world's radiation.

Years Ago

A night without their children;
The parents have been set free.
This once wild group, since humbled
By the countless poops and pee.

But tonight, they are unleashed,
Though no longer in their prime.
They may even go so far
As to stay up past bedtime!

Their only plan is excess drinking
To make up for years confined.
Years filled, not with beer and shots,
But sippy cups, bibs, and whine.

They get excited about the blender
Like they've never seen one before.
Giddy over ice and rum
And the fruity drinks galore.

They talk about their last night out –
Oh, some twenty years ago –
Of all the things they said and did
That their kids need never know.

The years ago, come rushing back
And the drinks are fast in flowing.
But soon enough, the tides will turn
And what was coming will be going.

So, as they retch the night away
And are feeling barely alive
The difference from those "years ago"
Is that the kids are up at five!

Spaced Out

While looking through my telescope
At the moon's many craters,
I'd swear that I saw a ski slope
With a skiing alligator.

I know there's no snow on the moon,
Nor alligators that ski,
And maybe I am just a loon,
But I can't help what I see.

He slalomed for at least a mile
And I looked at him with awe
Because this athletic reptile
Did so without a flaw.

This lunar hallucination
May prove that I've lost my mind
Because much like a frozen Haitian,
A skiing gator's hard to find.

High Flying

Because of a stupid bar bet
I drank twelve shots of bourbon,
Then bought a flying carpet
From a man wearing a turban.

The bet concerned a question
That was posed to all around,
And I made the suggestion
That the answer could be found.

The question was moronic,
But the challenge had been set.
So, I drank a gin and tonic
And proceeded to win the bet.

The next time this question's asked of me
I will have a sure reply:
"*That's* how drunk one would have to be
To think that a carpet could fly."

Bar Nun

She's slinging beers and taking names
In a room judged full of sinners.
She's noting all their bad habits –
Lots of losers but no winners.

This rowdy bunch she blesses
With wisdom, love, and wine.
And they reply in limerick
With a phrase far from divine.

She sees her clergy in the mix.
There's not a saint amongst that crew.
They drink hearty then grope and grab
In that same way they often do.

While it's not always black and white
When it comes to her perception.
She's sure this crowd's going to Hell
As a whole, without exception.

This is just space-filling

Nonsense you need not read.

Go about your business.

Turn the page to proceed.

Fallen on Deaf Ears

I haven't been able to hear
Since I was a very young child
Due to a defect in my ear
That could not be reconciled.

But usually, it is alright
Because I've learned how to read lips,
Unless they speak in dark of night
Or during a solar eclipse.

So yesterday I was walking
Across a very busy street.
Many people's lips were talking,
Most complained about the heat.

But then I saw a man exclaim
Something that was most absurd.
It was the most bizarre claim
That my eyes had ever heard.

He was shouting, "The sky is falling!"
And I thought it was a riddle
That caused this guy to be calling
Like a new age Chicken Little.

But he insisted that I look
As he pointed toward the sky.
So, the glance that I then took
Was to appease this crazy guy.

So, I looked up in the air
And was quite shocked to see
That sure enough it was there
Falling right on top of me.

That's when I heard a faint cry —
The first sound I'd heard in years —
But then that descending sky
Crushed both me and my ears.

Part 𝍸𝍷
Writers, Writing &

Astounding Intellect

Periodically

As my sentence comes to an end
I call upon my loyal friend
To signify a brand-new start
And to keep my sentences apart,
But today, my friend, I cannot find
And I'm left in a punctuation bind,
Where on this page could my period be?
It seems the subject and verb don't agree,
And the period's trying to get away,
Which leaves a run-on in my essay
Making all my thoughts conjoint
And exclamations with no point!
Yet another has defected
This page needs to be corrected,
By a comma, this one was stolen,
They joined to become a semicolon;
And since I no longer have this friend
I'll have to *tell* you this is the end

Hired Education

I bought my college diploma
From this guy living on the street.
His body had a strange aroma,
But I thought it was just the heat.

I took my new college degree
And went looking for a job.
I was very proud of me,
Though I looked much like a slob.

So, I got myself a brand-new suit
And went to an interview.
I said, "I went to an institute,
So, ninety thousand dollars will do."

He said, "Your degree is impressive,
like the way the ink smears.
It is, in fact, the most expressive
That I have seen in many years.

"And while your suit's quite handsome,
I can't hire you for this job
Because you graduated from
The University of Bob."

Write It Down

Last night, while in bed,
A thought came to me
For the finest novel
The world would ever see.

I knew I could write it,
Of this there was no doubt,
Because the idea was grand,
As I've just pointed out.

And feeling quite smug
With what I'd achieved
I laid my head down
To allow a reprieve.

I soon drifted off
And fell back to sleep
To leave to my mind
This great thought to keep.

And I dreamt many dreams
Filled with fortune and fame
Where everyone wanted
Me to sign my name,

And of all of the grants
And the prizes I'd win

For just writing down
What this thought would begin.

But when I awoke
The following day
I realized my thought
Had slipped far away.

I struggled for long
With a great deal of strain
And squeezed at my temples
To loosen my brain

In hopes that my thought
Would emerge once again,
So I could transfer it
From my mind to my pen.

Many months and years passed
And all that I learned
Was that my thought was lost
And would never return.

But I take this lesson
For the next time I think,
Which from now on I'm sure
To do written in ink.

Kindergarten Bad Ass

He defies the orders
Of crossing guards.
He can't be bothered
With teacher's flash cards.

He likes the pet hamster,
But prefers the snake,
And spends most of nap time
Staying awake.

He'll have no chocolate –
He takes his milk straight,
And often is seen
With a girl who is eight.

He runs with scissors.
He sniffs all the glues.
His body is covered
With press-on tattoos.

He usually colors
Outside the lines
And doesn't paint by numbers,
Just random designs.

He's not sure why the dish
Ran off with the spoon
And doesn't care to find out
Any time soon.

He's the one you'll notice;
A cut above his peers,
Though perhaps he should be,
Having been there three years.

A Hack Poet's Dilemma

I was crafting a most brilliant quatrain
With rhymes never rivaled in verse,
Which, as I brought toward its conclusion,
Took an unfortunate turn for the worse.

This poem, a destined masterpiece.
This final quatrain its culmination.
And as the pen touched to the paper
I could scant refrain from excitation.

The stanza was crisp and well metered.
Each word's selection pristine.
Yet the rhyme, in the end, proved elusive,
To wit, the short phrase "that chick's spleen."

Square Off

The teacher said, "Parallelogram,"
And I said with a flair,
"I must beg to differ ma'am,
That shape is just a square!"

I was quite proud of my choice
And expected to earn great praise,
But her burning eyes just sought the voice
That had said that foolish phrase.

She started coming toward me
With finger pointing, all the while.
And I must admit I tried to flee,
Only to trip in the aisle.

She picked me up and shook me
And punched me in the diaphragm.
She pointed and yelled, "What do you see?!"
And I said, "A parallelogram."

Something About Nothing

I know a lot about nothing
And nothing about a lot.
I know something for nothing
Is something that won't be got.

One thing leads to another
As long as anything goes
And the only thing that's everything
Is the thing that no one knows.

This is just something about nothing –
Nothing more than a waste of your time,
Because the thing or two I used to know
Is now something for another rhyme.

Distribution problem

He carved iambic pentameter
With a rock chisel and a smile.
And he seemed the disheveled artist,
Though that was just the style.

He was many millennia
Ahead of the progress of time.
His friends were all inaudible,
But *his* grunts were in rhyme.

The problem was once he finished,
And could share his works with all,
This Neanderthal of a poet
Found that he couldn't move the wall.

Phone Smart

This device once known
For its distinct dial tone
Has crippled me such
I can't think on my own.

I'm not sure when it happened
That my phone surpassed me,
But ever since I have earned
My "lazy genius" pedigree.

Now I need not know a thing –
My phone knows on my behalf.
Or it can tell a great joke,
Whenever I need a laugh.

It always has an answer
No matter what I need know,
Nor how foolish the question,
And without *quid pro quo.*

I'm witless without it
And feel anxious when parted,
But I know when I have it
I cannot be outsmarted.

So, I've come to realize
For my remaining lifespan
That I'm basically as good
As my presiding data plan.

The Periodic Tables Have Turned

The popular jock,
To whom the girls flock,
Inside this room is quite plain.
He's in science class
Where he's least badass
'Cause it's chemistry geek domain.

He thinks of touchdowns
And homecoming crowns
While his classmates point and guffaw.
They dream about Fission
And mock him with derision
When he can't cite Avogadro's Law.

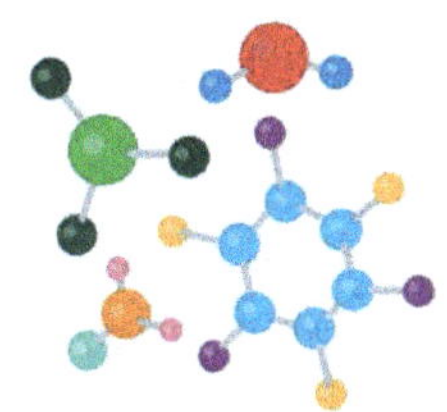

What he tries to learn
Makes their Bunsen's burn
To behold someone so inane.
They mix beakers and flasks
And complete all their tasks
While he crows, "My farts are methane."

Soon, they'll kick him out
And leave little doubt
That he's as brilliant as cement.
And he'll make a life change
To never again range
So far out of his element.

Retirement Village Mysteries: The Case of the Unraveled Shawl

The pile of yarn found on the couch
Had once been the shawl Millie knitted,
But now she sobbed alone in her room,
Asking how this crime was committed.

It was a puzzling mystery
Because it had come undone
While Millie went to the restroom,
Though, in her room, there was no one.

The cleaning crew was questioned,
As were her neighbors and friends.
Could this have been a message sent?
Did Millie need to make amends?

I sought out Millie's enemies,
But there were none to be found.
She was beloved by all she knew,
So, how did it become unwound?

I examined all the evidence,
Prepared to close the deal
Via the clue which told the tale –
A speck of yarn lint on her heel.

I used that to reconstruct the scene,
Caused by her urgent need to poo,
Which caused her to leave hastily
With the twine wrapped around her shoe.

A bad poet wrote a poem
Describing her own fart scent
And thus, was forced to report to
The Tortured Poets Department.

It was here they would assess
Her flaws and transgressions,
Where writer's had come before
To offer their confessions.

She was assigned to the top floor,
Where the worst offenders are seen.
The manager opened the room
Where they would poke, prod, and demean.

All that needed deciding was
The sentence that they would impose

Because her guilt was obvious
For the words she had used, she chose.

"You're accused of once rhyming
Using the very same words
Which is utterly absurd
And also completely absurd."

The evidence was all too clear,
So she was strung up by her feet
And forced to hear bad metaphors,
Like "that girl is Taylor Swift sweet."

A little waterboarding
Is not something at which they'd scoff,
So she will leave fully reformed
Unable to shake it off.

This is no place for the soulful
To work out their struggle and strife
But more for punishments rendered –
A poorly used pen gets the knife.

Should she revert to bad habits
And write a lazy limerick
Be assured TTPD
Will ensure it's dealt with quick.

Part 7
Odd Ends

Imagine That

I know imaginary people,
But can't really call them friends
Since they don't seem to like me,
Which is odd, since they're pretend.

These people, conjured by my mind,
Who I can think, but cannot touch,
Evidently have concluded
I'm not worth knowing very much.

I believe they've begun a movement
To plan secession from my brain.
These mutinous fake people
Are becoming a tangible pain.

There's nothing to do about it,
Unless perhaps there is a pill
That will liberate my mental state
And destroy their growing free will.

King Noone, the First

The smartest person
that ever I've known
Was a man who spent life
perched on a throne.

He possessed no regal
blood whatsoever,
Just simply a scheme
that was pretty damn clever.

He realized that people
want someone to revere
So, he offered an option
and made it quite clear.

He knew with a robe
and big fancy chair,
And speaking loudly
with a great deal of flair,

That because he wore
a crown on his head
Everyone would do
anything that he said.

And you know, he was right,
        and the riches rolled in
And no one ever asked
        who he was or had been.

So, the smartest person
        that ever I've known
Didn't get it from books,
        but all on his own.

He was just some guy
        with a crown and chair bling
Who one day chose
        to proclaim himself King.

Nature in a Box

My animal crackers were packaged
In what was a most peculiar way.
The animals seemed segregated
According to predator or prey.

Now, in a zoo, this makes good sense,
But as cracker packaging goes
I'm not sure it is necessary
To separate friends from foes.

In the normal course of fiction,
Such as in children's books or games,
Enemies live harmoniously,
And with crackers, I'd think the same.

Maybe I shouldn't take notice.
Perhaps it matters not in the least,
But I can't ignore the care taken
To separate lions from wildebeest.

So, I lift the box to examine,
But then drop the entire collection.
And the discord crushes them all
In my version of natural selection.

By Drill or Bicuspid

Drifting along the root canal
This anesthetized martyr,
Whose crown was lost some time ago,
Had lost the nerve to fight tartar.

His youthful predecessor
Was sold cheaply to a fairy
And when the wise quartet departed
He became increasingly wary.

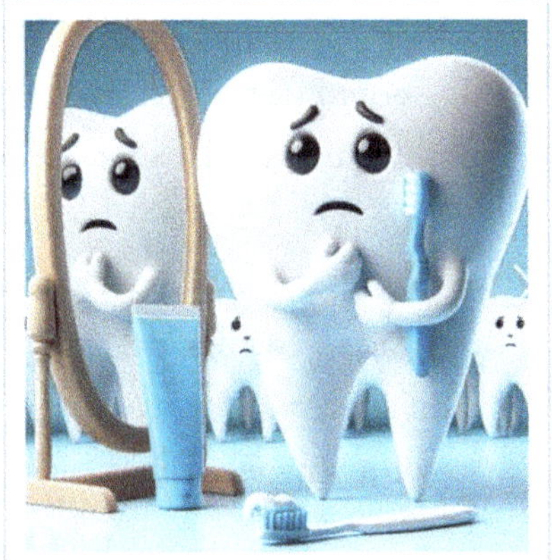

He saw the gums receding
And feared he was next to go.
None of the eyes saw a thing.
He could not tell friend from foe.

The plaque that he'd been given
Was hardly an honor at all.
Then he felt his grip loosen
And was sure of his own fall.

Christmas List

I went to the department store
To give Santa Claus my wish list,
But I got more than I bargained for
Because this Santa was a nudist.

I saw no belted big red suit,
Nor any small cone-shaped cap.
Then this Santa of ill-repute
Motioned for me to sit on his lap.

I tried to keep eye contact
As I slowly walked toward his chair,
But I could not avoid the fact
That this Santa Claus was bare.

He did indeed have rosy cheeks.
But I didn't further delve.
I didn't recover for weeks
From the image of buck-naked elves.

He stood beside the Christmas tree
With his ornaments hanging proud
And he gave out his gifts for free,
While shouting, "Ho, ho," real loud.

Throughout the store he mingled
And was somewhat more than jolly.
I'd say this aberrant Kris Kringle
Could have used some well-placed holly.

Since then, my list has changed because
Christmas was ruined for this year.
Now all I want's for Santa Claus
To be trampled by his reindeer.

The Prick I Am

If you were blind
I'd say, "Look at me."
If you were in jail
I'd say, "It's nice to be free."

Lying dogs are for kicking.
There's no treat worth not tricking.

I'd say, "Just go home,"
To a wandering lost soul.
If I were Santa Claus
I'd give only coal.

Cripples, midgets and retards
Are fodder for laughing real hard.

I'd scream, "Bombs away!"
To a shell-shocked vet.
I'd trip a high wire act
Who walked without a net.

When an old person falls ill
I try to get into their will.

That's just the prick I am
And I'm not going to change.
I'll make fun of you
If you're the least bit strange.

There's no more for me to say or do
And so, with that, I'm done with you.

Barber Chair Blues

I get the barber chair blues
Over the hairs that I lose
Every time I sit in that chair.
The scissors are unkind
To my receding hairline,
Leaving me practically bare.

Oh, those barber chair blues
Are my only excuse
For not going to the barbershop,
Because when I hear the shears
It brings me to tears
To know I'm losing more off the top.

Well, I have got some bad news
For those barber chair blues:
I soon will have no hair on my head.
Then I will put a hat on
And all my blues will be gone.
I'll be a happy bald man instead.

Clonely

I wish that I could be cloned,
So there could be more of me.
Then I would never be alone,
Which would fill my hearts with glee.

After *I* became *us*
We'd be happy all the time.
And like the rich and famous
We would work for not a dime.

I could just send one of me
To rob a local store,
Then I would get the money
And he'd get two to four.

Then I could make another
To take that lost clone's place.
I would say we were brothers,
Each with the exact same face.

The greatest thing of all would be
At once, I could be everywhere
Because it would be amazing to see
Myself both here and there.

Joe's Circus

Big Top Joe
And his one-man show
Have come to this nearby town,
But all I see
Is a guy like me
Who dresses up like a clown.

Ringmaster Joe
Is the whole show
Because there are no others there.
I paid the bucks,
But this show sucks.
He's just a guy with a whip and chair.

High wire Joe
Stands on his toe
Hundreds of feet in the air,
But no crowd's around
To watch this lone clown
And I can't pretend that I care.

Soon high-flying Joe
Will be just a side show
Because his trapeze act is weak,
For he hasn't thought
About how he'll be caught
And will be left a distorted freak.

A Gravedigger's Lament

All that I can say
Is it was my first day
And the markings were not very clear.
So, when I reached the spot
I thought was the plot
The actions I took were sincere.

I quick dug the hole,
As had been my goal,
And paid homage by tipping my hat.
But I had dug where
A grave had been there,
And you're not supposed to do that.

Then it happened again,
And again for all ten,
Till the sun rose and I knew my mistakes.
Then the mourners came
And found me to blame
For compounding all their heartbreaks.

I calmed them down, though,
And climbed on my backhoe
And said, "*I can make this all right.*
If you could just claim
the ones with your name
I can have them put back by tonight."

But this now angry mob
Didn't want to hobnob,
And preferred to bury *me* deep.
They took over my rig
And started to dig
Then left me beneath the new heap.

Retirement Village Mysteries: The Case of the Stolen Dentures

In our midst, a crime has been committed.
With respect to our noses, it happened beneath.
And while I, myself, can be acquitted,
Still, someone has stolen my grandpa's false teeth.

But it occurs to me that the transgressor
Has likely left behind many clues
That, while it's short of a confessor,
Will lead to the one that we should accuse.

With a quick perusal of his room
I see a trail of urine leading out
That if we follow, it's safe to assume,
Will take us to the thief's hideout.

Quickly, I can deduce the scheme,
Which began with a fight that made him madder
Than his body could take, so it would seem,
And so he lost control of his bladder.

Then this thief, who was at least eighty,
Took the teeth, leaving this trail behind.
And that person is Old Man Brady
In whose mouth those teeth I'm sure you'll find.

The Ol' Clickbait Hard Sell

Hurry up and click it fast.
Please do not be late.
I need my fractional penny,
So take no time to debate.

The link's right there, so go ahead,
There is no time to waste.
You surely don't want to miss,
So do so now, with haste.

FOMO must be creeping in,
But time is running out.
Your last chance is coming now
To see what it's all about.

Oh no, you waited too long!
It's gone till who knows when.
But perhaps just for you
I could post it once again.

Desserted

You were stranded, left all alone,
But learned it was no time to cry
When you discovered the waffle cone
With ice cream piled three feet high.

You should have sent a signal flare
To call for rescue from this place
But instead had a piece of cake
And some pie from the sugar case.

A search party sounded like fun
Until you found for your protection
They'd remove you from your island
And leave behind its confections.

But once you ditched them in the end,
And were forever free from crowds,
To spend your days without a friend
'Neath gumdrop trees and whipped cream clouds

You reached a state of eternal bliss,
Under toffee canopy sheath.
With donuts and a chocolate kiss
You'll love life with both your teeth.

Caterwauling

I've been eyeballing
The creature that's crawling
And desperately bawling
'cause it is appalling.

And I cried out calling
Once it started falling.
My ass was quick hauling.
'Twas no time for stalling.

If I don't come brawling
It soon will be mauling
And I'll be sent sprawling
And speaking half-drawling.

Its presence is galling,
So it is enthralling
The traps I'm installing.
I hope they're forestalling.

Magic Show

I pulled a rabbit from my hat
And many cheers were attained,
But I didn't know that
Still inside that hat
That rabbit's feces remained.

After the show, I left that place
And I put that hat on my head,
But then the disgrace
And the look on my face
Was a story that quickly spread.

Because of that little white hare
I no longer perform magic,
For I am too scared
That once more I'll wear
His poop, and that is just tragic.

Alien Abduction Reject

They beamed me up into their ship,
Prepared to poke and prod,
When I noticed their strange faces
Looked at me like *I* was odd.

They talked amongst themselves
And returned, shaking their heads.
Somehow, I wasn't good enough
For the probes beside the beds.

"You didn't really fit our need,"
They said inside my mind.
"You're not what we're looking for
To represent mankind."

They didn't even beam me back,
Just shoved me from their craft,
And as I fell down to the ground
They watched me fall and laughed.

There must have been confusion.
I'm a fine specimen, I'd say.
At least, that's what my shrink tells me
When I say they'll be back someday.

Info Dump

During Valsalva Maneuver,
When my mind is most apt to bear down,
My face takes on an expression
Of epiphany inside a frown.

A push for more information
Helps me focus when I might strain,
As I finish my thoughts before
All my effort goes down the drain.

The thoughts I conceive are wondrous
With knowledge that I have to share,
Though I find I'm often solo
When I'm on the porcelain chair.

A Whiff of Royalty

The monarchy was in a bind
With a problem not to be confined,

Because the shifting wind that blew
Would reveal the secret they all knew,

But had concealed from all the rest –
All kingdoms found from east to west –

That their small country's beloved queen
Was one who practiced bad hygiene.

Of course, no one had the nerve to tell
The queen about her horrid smell

So the problem had gone on a while
With the state in collective denial.

But the time had come that they long feared
Her aroma was released unsteered,

Her odor drifting on its way
Across the land and toward the bay

To be unleashed upon the world,
A thousand lunches would be hurled.

According to media leaks
She hadn't bathed for many weeks

And wasn't one to properly wipe
So she was especially ripe,

With a strong and unrivaled funk
That made the crowds adore a skunk,

Thus the harsh reality, methinks –
People embarrassed that their queen stinks.

But what would soon be known to all,
Little did they know, would save their fall.

For you see, on a northbound course
There was a large invasion force,

A powerful army marching ahead
Intent to leave them sacked and dead,

But that force's advance was halted
When their noses were assaulted,

And the invaders were turned away
Ne'er to return another day,

For they had faced a horrible stench
That caused all their stomachs to wrench.

Then her subjects gleefully shrieked
Since they were saved because she reeked,

And everyone then screamed "Huzzah!"
And knew from wealthy to bourgeois

That their fair lady's putrid scents
Were, in fact, their best defense.

Part 8

These are for the Horseracing & Gambling Degenerates

For Bettor, or Worse

I bet the Win, not the Show,
But my "winner" was slow –
Heart stops;
Stomach drops –
Now back to the window.

Double Dribble Entendre

I was having sex with my girl
But had the game on my mind,
Since while I held onto hers
My team had fallen behind.

As they both progressed along,
They were different types of grind,
Till a back door cover got me,
And I don't mean the good kind.

Slot Machine Junkie Rap

I feel the reels
Bringing wins
Or bonus spins
While it steals
From the rest.
Progressive's hot,
A big jackpot,
That's no jest.

The payline hits
On a wild.
I get riled,
But don't quit
Pumpin' dimes.
Across the lines
The light's shine
For sharp rhymes.

Then slots go tight.
Bankroll fades.
Won't get paid.
Pockets gone light.

Lady luck's path
Keeps me chasing,
Can't be facing
My wife's wrath

Play till dawn,

Freezing machines

Runs my cash lean –

It's all gone.

House wins again,

I can't fix,

No bag of tricks.

Don't know when I'll go home.

Feelin' ill

Wife might kill,

So I'll just roam.

Rob the cashier,

Head to jail,

Don't want bail,

I'll just stay here.

Running A *Whole* Race is Exhausting

Our blazing-fast colt
Jumps out to the lead.
The field vainly gives chase.
It must be in the breed.

Hits his typical mark
Well in front of them all,
And the track announcer's roll
Leads with his name called.

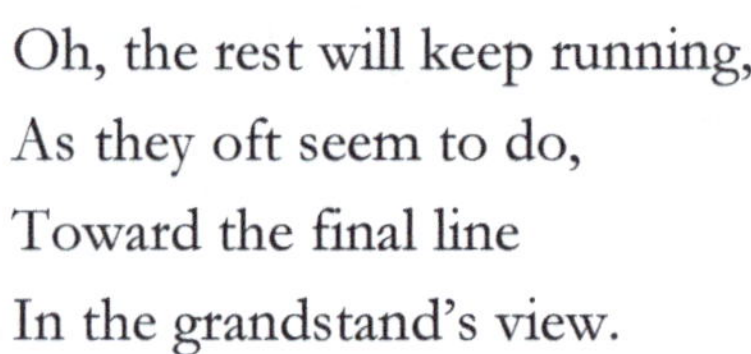

Oh, the rest will keep running,
As they oft seem to do,
Toward the final line
In the grandstand's view.

But our guy's easing up.
He has gone far enough,
Since he knows that home stretch
Can be kind of rough.

We don't need the win picture –
We know how he looks –
As our three-furlong champ
Puts one more in the books.

Wild Cards on the Table

Three-card monte on the playground.
None of these kids stand a chance.
I'll take them for their lunch money,
Despite their parents' sideways glance.

"Find the Queen," I say with a smirk,
"Before it's time for me to leave."
Then a pigtailed six-year-old says,
"I see you hid it up your sleeve."

For a moment, I stare her down,
And no one around makes a sound,
Then I snatch up my cards and run,
While shoving kids to the ground.

My getaway's never graceful
When a brainy kid thwarts my trick,
But at least I'll sleep well knowing
That the charges will never stick.

Retirement Village Mysteries: The Case of the Bingo Charlatan

I called out "O, fifty-four,"
And Betty yelled it once again.
She had scored another "Bingo!"
That was eight times out of ten.

There were murmurs amongst the crowd,
Suspicion beginning to grow.
"How was it Betty won so much?"
Everyone there wanted to know.

But she just smiled pleasantly
With her marker poised in her hand,
Though something in her grin foretold
That it all was somehow planned.

Her husband clapped beside the stage
Each time that she marked her card,
And I looked at him skeptically
Like the game they played was marred.

When Betty won yet again,
Which made it nine of eleven,
Esther and Gladys each made a fist –
Ready to send Betty to Heaven.

That's when the entire scheme struck me
And I moved to intervene
Because I noticed the husband
Was the one keeping the balls clean.

So upon close examination
I found the way the number falls
Was determined by a contrived weight,
Courtesy of hubby's brass balls.

A Horse With Some Name

"And they're off," he announced
In his slick baritone;
His signature sound
That made each call his own.

The speed straight to the lead,
As he knew would take place,
But he called out a name
From the previous race.

He shook off the mistake
And refocused his eyes
Then listed the field
To a great deal of surprise.

For the names he exclaimed,
As they sprinted the lawn,
Were horses from races,
Not the race going on.

The crowd wondered a bit
And looked at their sheets,
But when the long shot won
They roared in their seats.

And for the rest of the day
All insisted he call
Each horse by a name
That no one knew at all.

THE

END

And the Joke's on You

Having now reached the end
Of wasted time better spent
I can't help but surmise
What you thought its intent

When you first saw on the shelf,
And then clearly mistook,
This bound collection
For a somewhat worthwhile book.

And I'm sure you opened it
Quite enthused to begin
To partake in rare wisdom
Found on the pages within.

But as you proceeded
And thought, "*This is inane,*"
And the term "*useless garbage*"
Became your refrain
You realized that it truly
Offered nothing to gain.

But I, the "writer," do know,
And now humbly profess,
That you, the reader, are key
To my ongoing success,

So take solace in that
This book was made well,
With crisp, sturdy pages*
And, I think, a nice smell.

*(*E-book readers please alternatively note the 3D effects when you cross your eyes)*

You think I'm a moron.
You think I'm a tool,
And likely other names
That are equally as cruel,
But *you're* the one who bought it,
So now who is the fool?

This is the Participation Part of the Program

If you laughed even once
As you read to the end
Write a real nice review
And I'll be your best friend.*

**It would violate publication policy and all moral codes to tie the offer of enduring friendship to your providing a positive review of this book, so of course, there is no obligation.* [JK – write a damn review!]

About the "Author"

Tony Esposito writes words because he can, not because he's "good at it" or someone who should "quit his day job" or somebody with a "what the f**k's wrong with you" personality disorder.

Some of the poems in this book date back more than 30 years, while others were written within the past year. He thinks that kind of consistency in moronic foolishness is an accomplishment few could achieve (his four daughters attest to the high bar his nonsense quotient can reach).

He wrote some children's books before, but nobody bought them, so why not thrust more unwanted content on the world?

Anyway, TL;DR – Tony Esposito is old, unaccomplished, and perhaps a fool, but the book's still great, in his opinion. More to come. You haven't seen anything yet.

www.ingramcontent.com/pod-product-compliance
Lightning Source LLC
Chambersburg PA
CBHW071127100726
47908CB00008B/2510